A Note to Parents and Teachers

DK READERS is a compelling program for beginning readers, designed in conjunction with leading literacy experts, including Dr. Linda Gambrell, Professor of Education at Clemson University. Dr. Gambrell has served as President of the National Reading Conference and the College Reading Association, and has recently been elected to serve as President of the International Reading Association.

Beautiful illustrations and superb full-color photographs combine with engaging, easy-to-read stories to offer a fresh approach to each subject in the series.

Each DK READER is guaranteed to capture a child's interest while developing his or her reading skills, general knowledge, and love of reading.

The five levels of DK READERS are aimed at different reading abilities, enabling you to choose the books that are exactly right for your child:

Pre-level 1: Learning to read
Level 1: Beginning to read
Level 2: Beginning to read alone
Level 3: Reading alone
Level 4: Proficient readers

The "normal" age at which a child begins to read can be anywhere from three to eight years old. Adult participation through the lower levels is very helpful for providing encouragement, discussing storylines, and sounding out unfamiliar words.

No matter which level you select, you can be sure that you are helping your child learn to read, then read to learn!

LONDON, NEW YORK, MUNICH,
MELBOURNE, AND DELHI

Editor Kate Simkins
Designers Cathy Tincknell
and John Kelly
Senior Editor Catherine Saunders
Brand Manager Lisa Lanzarini
Publishing Manager Simon Beecroft
Category Publisher Alex Allan
DTP Designer Hanna Ländin
Production Rochelle Talary
Reading Consultant Linda Gambrell

First American Edition, 2007
Published in the United States by
DK Publishing
375 Hudson Street
New York, New York 10014

07 08 09 10 10 9 8 7 6 5 4 3 2 1

Copyright © 2007 Dorling Kindersley Limited

Published in Great Britain by Dorling Kindersley Limited.

DK books are available at special discounts for bulk purchases for
sales promotion, premiums, fund-raising, or educational use.
For details contact: DK Publishing Special Markets,
375 Hudson Street, New York, NY 10014

A Cataloging-in-Publication record for this book is available from
the Library of Congress.

ISBN 978-0-7566-2563-4 (paperback)
ISBN 978-0-7566-2564-1 (hardcover)

All artwork by Inklink except the illustrations of the town, the
temple, and the pharaoh on page 42, the servant, marriage contract,
prisoners, Chief Embalmer, and Lord Ini's Palace on page 43, the
pyramid, burial chamber, and the robbers on page 44, the soldiers
and the House of the Dead on page 45, the priest and the temple on
page 46, and the natron table on page 48 by Richard Bonson.

Discover more at
www.dk.com

Contents

DK READERS

PROFICIENT **4** READERS

CURSE of the CROCODILE GOD

Written by Stewart Ross
Illustrated by Inklink

DK Publishing

CURSE OF THE CROCODILE GOD

Methen's story takes place 4,000 years ago in Ancient Egypt. It is the year 1795 BCE, and the ruler of Egypt is Pharaoh Sobekneferu. Our hero and his new friend Madja live in a town near Hawara in northern Egypt. Turn to page 42 to see a map of Ancient Egypt and a timeline, then let the story begin....

"MY NAME IS METHEN, and this is my friend Madja. Our lives are in great danger! We are caught in a fiendish plot hatched by a corrupt official. As the son of a respected priest, nothing in my life has prepared me for this. My days have been spent at scribe school, learning to read and write. Madja is a servant girl in a nobleman's court. Like me, she is 13 years old, but our paths had never crossed until the evening of the banquet at Lord Ini's palace."

THE SILVER MOON LIT OUR WAY ACROSS THE DESERT AS MY FATHER LED ME INTO **TOWN**.

I NEVER EVEN WANTED TO GO.

FATHER MADE ME.

IT IS THE WISH OF LORD INI TO MEET YOU, METHEN.

Words in **bold** appear in the glossary on page 42.

DID YOU KNOW? *The land of Ancient Egypt was in North Africa.*

DID YOU KNOW? *Most Ancient Egyptian towns were surrounded by high wa*

DID YOU KNOW? *The first Egyptian pyramid was built in 2650 BCE.*

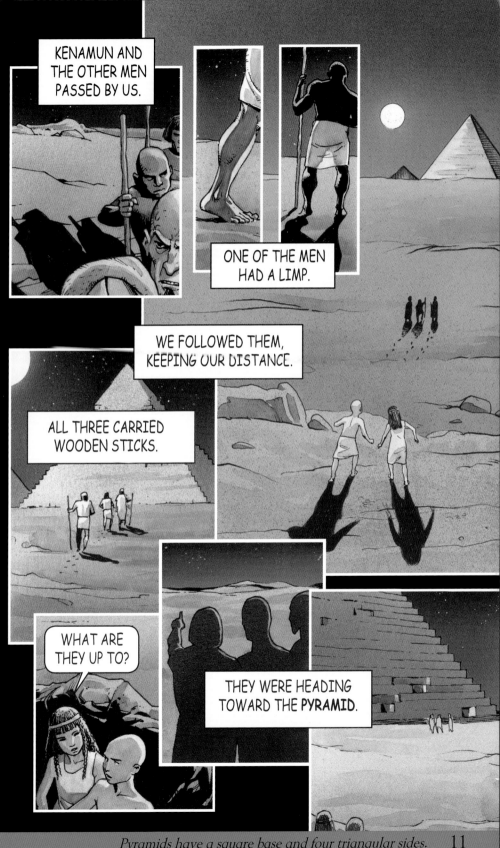

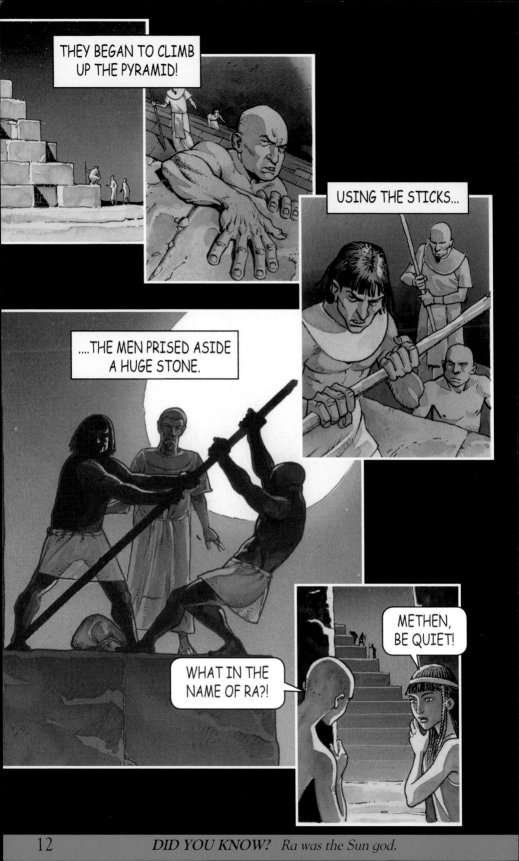

DID YOU KNOW? Ra was the Sun god.

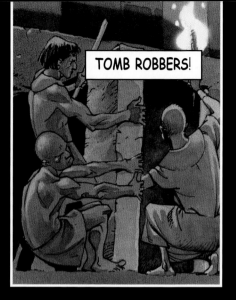

TOMB ROBBERS!

THEY VANISHED INTO THE PYRAMID!

LET'S FOLLOW!

MADJA, LOOK!

IT WAS A SECRET PASSAGEWAY LEADING INTO THE PYRAMID.

THE PASSAGEWAY WAS HOT AND DARK. THE AIR WAS STALE.

The Great Pyramid was made of more than 2 million stone blocks.

DID YOU KNOW? *Pyramids had trap doors to capture robbers.*

DID YOU KNOW? The burial chambers were full of treasure.

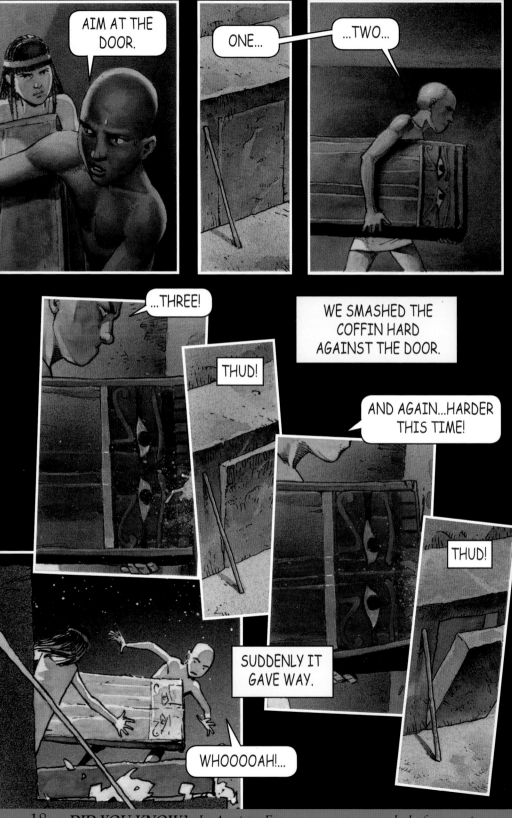

DID YOU KNOW? In Ancient Egypt, eyes were a symbol of protection.

DID YOU KNOW? It took 70 days to make a mummy.

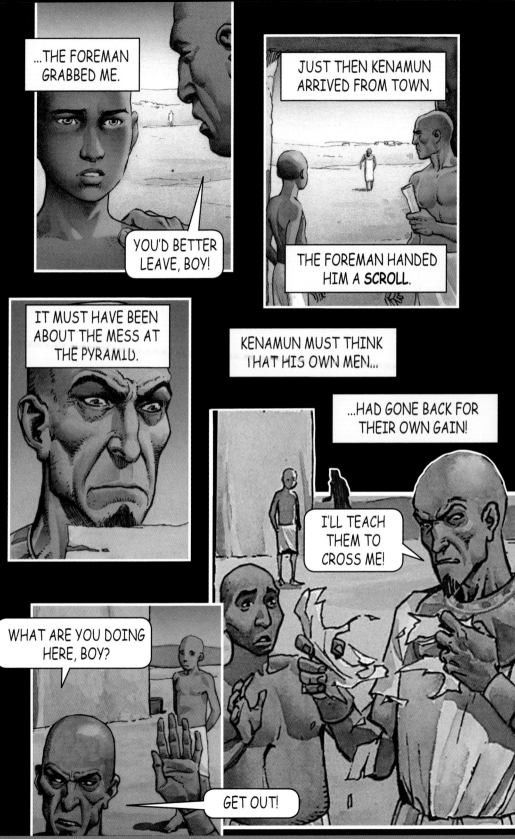

Anubis was the god of embalming (making mummies).

NEXT MORNING, I WENT TO WORK WITH FATHER.

HE IS A **PRIEST** IN THE TEMPLE OF SOBEK.

THE CURSE OF SOBEK LAY HEAVY ON MY HEAD!

I HAD TO ASK FATHER ABOUT THE FATE OF THE PYRAMID THIEVES.

I WAITED WHILE HE PREPARED THE **OFFERINGS.**

THE RITUALS SEEMED TO TAKE FOREVER.

DID YOU KNOW? *Sobek was half man, half crocodile.*

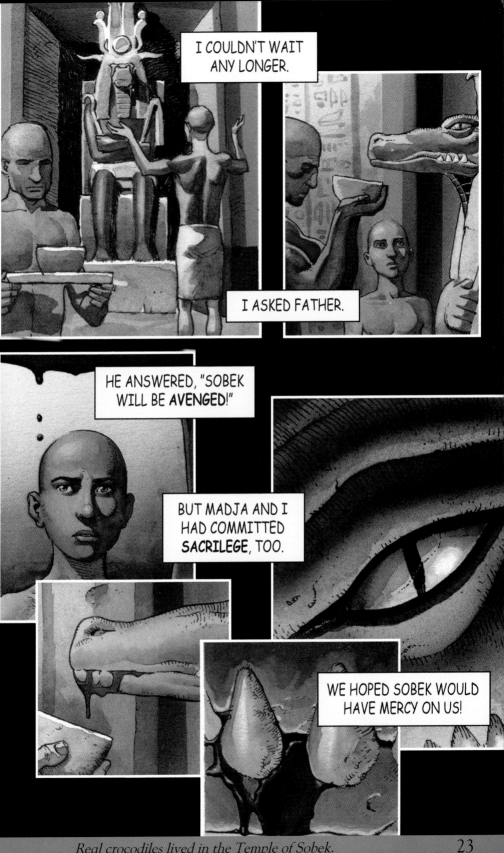

Real crocodiles lived in the Temple of Sobek.

DID YOU KNOW? Ancient Egypt grew up alongside the Nile River.

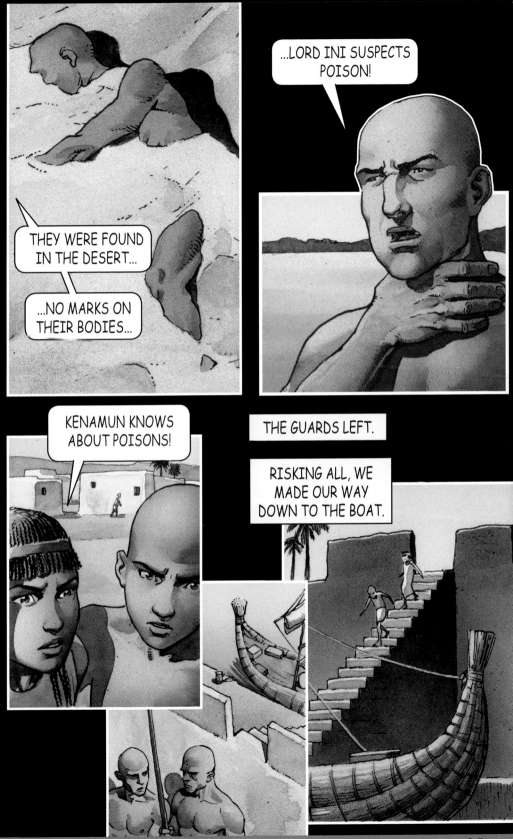

DID YOU KNOW? The Nile River flooded every year.

The river was full of dangerous animals such as crocodiles and hippos.

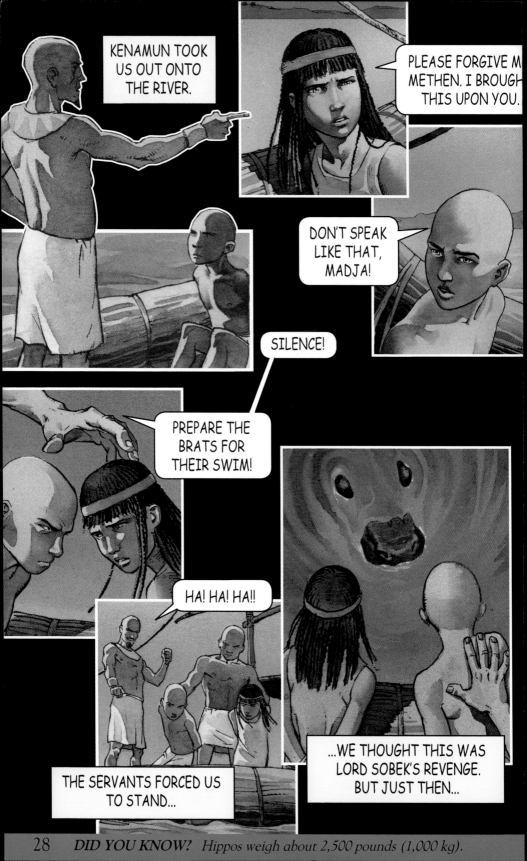

DID YOU KNOW? *Hippos weigh about 2,500 pounds (1,000 kg).*

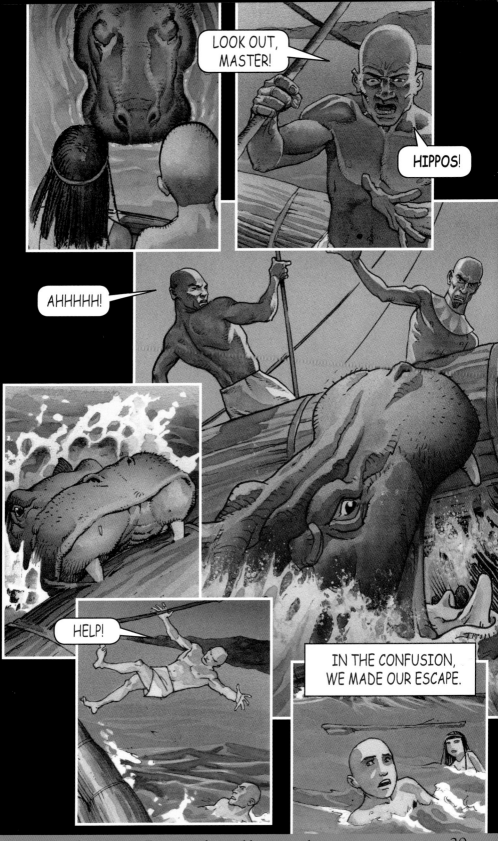

The Ancient Egyptians hunted hippos with spears. 29

DID YOU KNOW? *Papyrus grows up to 10 feet (3 meters) tall.*

DID YOU KNOW? Sobekneferu was a female pharaoh.

WHEN KENAMUN ARRIVED, HE DENIED EVERYTHING.

IT IS A SHAMEFUL FALSEHOOD, YOUR MAJESTY! WHERE IS THE EVIDENCE?

I SWEAR BY SOBEK THAT WE ARE HONEST.

WHY WAS IAHAMES KILLED, SIRE?

DID HE KNOW TOO MUCH?

IGNORANT SLAVE! SLAY HER!

DID YOU KNOW? *The Ancient Egyptians called Egypt "Kemet."*

DID YOU KNOW? Natron was used for drying out bodies.

Mummies were wrapped in up to 20 layers of bandages.

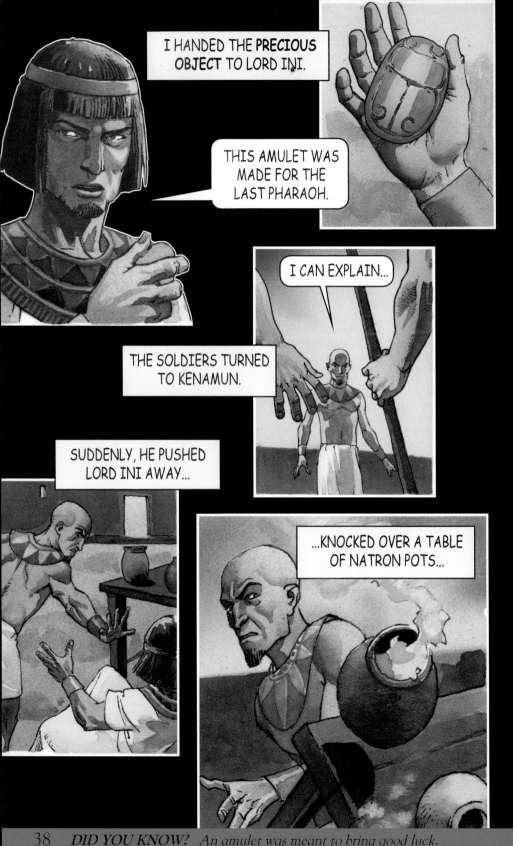

DID YOU KNOW? *An amulet was meant to bring good luck.*

DID YOU KNOW? *Small reed boats were pushed along with poles.*

King Menes unites Egypt	Pharaoh Sobekneferu comes to the throne	Death of Pharaoh Rameses III
3100	c. 1799	1153

3000 BCE (BEFORE COMMON ERA)   2000 BCE   YOU ARE HERE   1000 BCE

ANCIENT EGYPT

Ancient Egypt flourished in North Africa from about 4000 BCE to 332 CE. It grew up on a strip of fertile land, never more than a few miles wide, that lay on either side of the Nile River. Fed by rains falling to the south, the Nile snakes through the African desert until it reaches the Mediterranean Sea.

Great Pyramid at Giza
Memphis
Hawara
EGYPT
RIVER NILE
Thebes
Valley of the Kings

GLOSSARY

TOWN   PAGE 5

Most towns in Ancient Egypt were crowded with many houses, crammed together in unplanned streets.
The houses were made of mud bricks baked in the sun.

PHARAOH   PAGE 6

At the top of Egyptian society was the king called a pharaoh. He was considered a god by the Egyptians and above the normal rules of society. Most pharaohs were men, but a few women ruled Ancient Egypt at different times.

Female pharaoh Hatshepsut

SOBEK TEMPLE   PAGE 6

Sobek was the crocodile god. He was praised all over Egypt in temples, where priests guarded, cared for, and worshipped the god's image day and night. The priests even prepared meals for the god.

Picture of Sobek on the temple wall

Roman Empire collapsing		Columbus sails to America	US astronauts land on the Moon
410		1492	1969

TIMELINE

1 CE (COMMON ERA)　　　　　1000 CE　　　　　2000 CE

MARRIAGE　　　　PAGE 9

Most marriages in Ancient Egypt were arranged by the girl's father and mother. Girls would marry at around 13 years of age and boys at 16.
A scribe could draw up a contract giving equal rights to husband and wife.

Groom　　Bride　　Scribe

Prisoners of war

SERVANT　　　PAGE 8

Madja is a servant who works for Lord Ini. Servants were often prisoners brought to Egypt from other countries during wars. They were made to work for rich people and had no rights or freedom.

Servant

CHIEF EMBALMER　　　PAGE 7

The Chief Embalmer was in charge of mummifying bodies to preserve them. The Ancient Egyptians believed this helped people live forever. The Chief Embalmer wore a jackal's mask that symbolized Anubis, the god of the dead.

Chief Embalmer

LORD INI'S PALACE　　　PAGE 9

Lord Ini was a rich nobleman who lived in a large palace. The house was expensively decorated, and the interior walls were brightly painted with pictures of people, ducks, and lotus flowers (a type of lily).

43

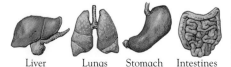
Liver   Lungs   Stomach   Intestines

ENTRAILS   PAGE 9

The entrails are the internal organs of
a dead person, such as the intestines.
These were removed when a body was
mummified and stored in special jars.

The Great Pyramid

The burial chamber

PYRAMID   PAGE 11

The pyramids were burial tombs for
the pharaohs and their queens. The
biggest one ever built was the Great
Pyramid built during the reign of
Pharaoh Khufu (2589–2566 BCE).

TOMB ROBBERS   PAGE 13

The pyramids were full of valuable
things that the pharaoh might need in
the afterlife. Although the tombs had
secret passages and rooms, they were
easy for robbers to dig their way into.

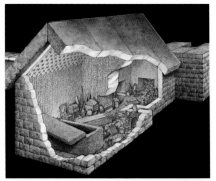

BURIAL CHAMBER   PAGE 15

The body of the pharaoh was buried in
the burial chamber hidden deep inside
the pyramid. Its whereabouts were
meant to be a secret, but since many
helped build the temple, the room was
often easy for robbers to find.

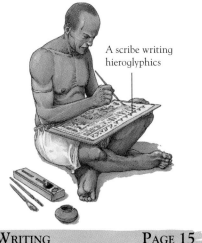

A scribe writing
hieroglyphics

WRITING   PAGE 15

Ancient Egyptian writing was a type
of picture writing called hieroglyphics.
Only scribes like Methen could read
and write.

COFFIN   PAGE 17

The mummy was placed in a wooden coffin case that was often shaped like a person. The coffin was often painted with pictures and hieroglyphics.

Mummy wrapped in bandages

MUMMIES   PAGE 20

The embalmed bodies of the dead were called mummies. After they were dried out and the organs removed, the bodies were usually wrapped in bandages.

Coffin case

SOLDIERS   PAGE 20

Soldiers were workers forced to serve the pharaoh. They carried spears and shields but wore little armor.

SCROLL   PAGE 21

Scribes wrote on sheets of papyrus paper that were rolled up into scrolls. Papyrus was a plant that grew beside the Nile River.

HOUSE OF THE DEAD   PAGE 20

Dead bodies were mummified in the House of the Dead in a ritual that lasted 70 days. They were dried so that they did not rot and then usually wrapped in bandages.

Soldier   General

Priest

PRIEST   PAGE 22
Priests like Methen's
father performed
important religious
ceremonies, or rituals.
They were important
people in Egyptian life.

OFFERINGS   PAGE 22
The priests prepared food and other
offerings for the gods. Sobek, the
crocodile god, was offered honey
cakes and meat.

Only the priests could
approach the shrine of Sobek

AVENGED   PAGE 23
Methen's father believes the god
Sobek will harm the pyramid thieves
in return for their wrongdoing, which
means Sobek will be avenged.

SACRILEGE   PAGE 23
Offending a god is called sacrilege.
Methen and Madja believe they
offended the god Sobek by entering
the pyramid and breaking a coffin.
They believe they were cursed by him.

BOAT   PAGE 24
Nile boats were made of bundles of
papyrus reeds. Cargo boats
transported heavy goods
such as building stone.

Papyrus cargo boat

Stone being
transported

THE NILE   PAGE 24
The civilization of Ancient Egypt
depended on the Nile River. Every
year, the river flooded the surrounding
countryside, making the land better
for growing crops when the
water receded.

Farmland

Town

Nile at its
highest level

Flood water

Nile River

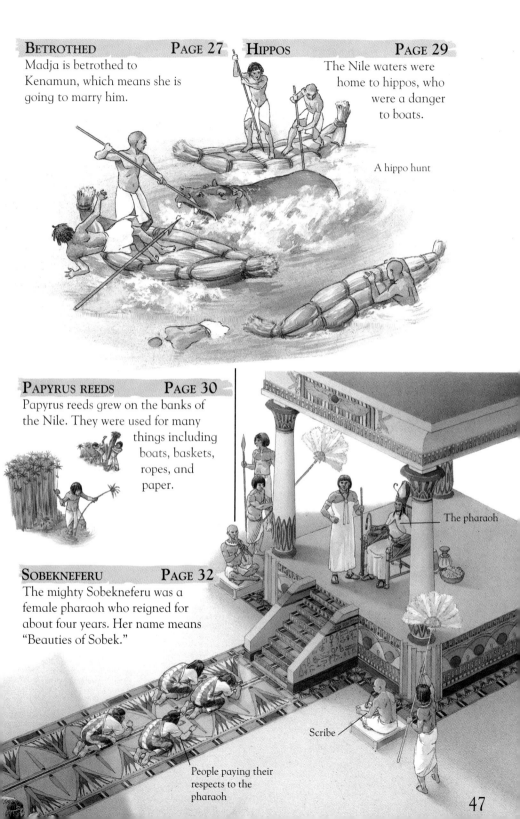

BETROTHED   PAGE 27

Madja is betrothed to Kenamun, which means she is going to marry him.

HIPPOS   PAGE 29

The Nile waters were home to hippos, who were a danger to boats.

A hippo hunt

PAPYRUS REEDS   PAGE 30

Papyrus reeds grew on the banks of the Nile. They were used for many things including boats, baskets, ropes, and paper.

SOBEKNEFERU   PAGE 32

The mighty Sobekneferu was a female pharaoh who reigned for about four years. Her name means "Beauties of Sobek."

The pharaoh

Scribe

People paying their respects to the pharaoh

47

Natron powder being
poured on a dead body

PRECIOUS OBJECT   PAGE 38

Precious objects, such as the amulet
Methen found, were valuable items.
They were put in the tomb in case
the pharaoh needed them in
the afterlife.

This necklace is
a precious object

NATRON   PAGE 36

Natron was a saltlike substance used
to dry out dead bodies when they were
being made into mummies. The white
powder was mined from dry lake beds
near the Nile River.

HORUS   PAGE 40

Horus was
an Egyptian
god with a
hawk's head.
The Horus-
eye was a
symbol of
healing and
protection.

A Horus-eye

EXECUTION   PAGE 36

The most common punishment in
Egypt was beating, but serious crimes
could be punished by execution, which
means being put to death.

Prisoners being beaten

OSIRIS   PAGE 41

Osiris was the god
of death and rebirth.
He judged the dead
in the Underworld.
Only those
who had led
good lives
were
granted
eternal
life.

Osiris and his
wife Isis

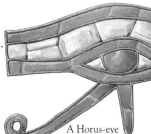

Horus

48